GREEN LIGHT FOR THE
LITTLE RED TRAIN

Benedict Blathwayt

HUTCHINSON
London Sydney Auckland Johannesburg

Duffy Driver and the Little Red Train arrived at the station to pick up their passengers.

"There's repair work
further up the line,"
said Jack the guard. "You'll
be following a different route
today. Keep going as long as the
lights are green."
"Right," said Duffy.

Sure enough, the points on the railway tracks sent Duffy one way and then another.

The line carried them down into a dark tunnel.

Duffy didn't realize
they were under
the sea!

When they came out at the other end,
the signal shone green so Duffy and the
Little Red Train kept going.

Duffy didn't realize he was in France.
Shouldn't I be back on my usual tracks
by now? he thought.

When they reached the next station, Duffy slowed down to ask what was going on.

But a noisy electric train clanked up behind them.
PEEP . . . PEEP . . . PEEP, it whistled.
  "Oh, go blow a fuse!" grumbled Duffy, and the
Little Red Train picked up speed again.

Duffy had no idea that he was now in Spain.
But the lights were still green so the Little Red
Train flew along at a tremendous rate.
   Clicketty clicketty clicketty clack

They went so fast and the sun was so hot that the Little Red Train's water tanks ran dry and the needle on the pressure gauge pointed to DANGER.

"Water!" shouted Duffy, putting on the brake. "We need water or the train will explode!"

Luckily there was water just ahead.
Everyone jumped down and helped
to fill the Little Red Train's water tanks.
TOOT . . . TOOT . . . TOOT, tooted
an impatient freight train behind them.
"Oh, nuts and bolts to you!" hissed Duffy.
But the signal far down the line shone
green so off they had to go again.

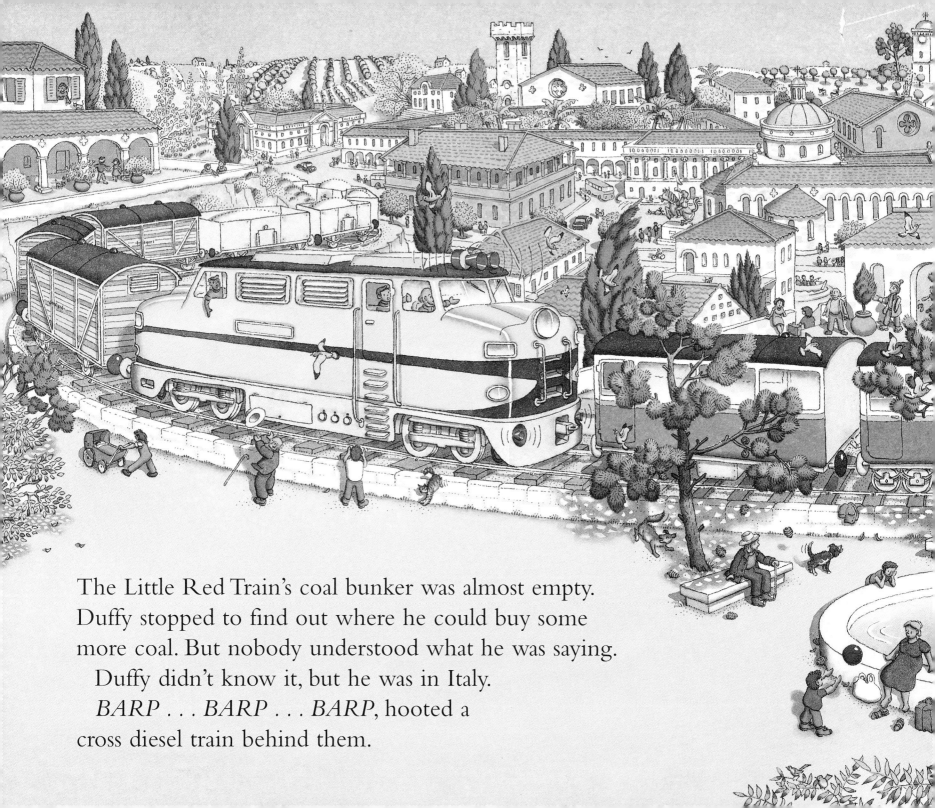

The Little Red Train's coal bunker was almost empty.
Duffy stopped to find out where he could buy some
more coal. But nobody understood what he was saying.

Duffy didn't know it, but he was in Italy.

BARP . . . BARP . . . BARP, hooted a
cross diesel train behind them.

"Oh, go pop your rivets!" shouted Duffy.
     But the signal lights glowed green so Duffy blew
the whistle and let off the brake and they were
soon speeding along again at a sizzling pace.
Whoo . . . ooo . . . eee
Chuffitty chuffitty chuffitty chuff

When the last lump of coal was gone, the fire in the firebox went out and the Little Red Train stopped.

"We're stuck!" cried Duffy.

So everyone jumped down and gathered dry wood until the Little Red Train's coal bunker was full.

But . . .

. . . HOO . . . HOO . . . HOO, honked a furious express train behind them.

"Oh, smoke and smuts to you!" yelled Duffy.

He lit a new fire in the firebox and soon the Little Red Train had built up enough steam to get going again.

This is the longest detour I've ever had to take, thought Duffy. But he had no idea just how far north he had come. He opened the throttle as wide as it would go and the Little Red Train's wheels spun and the wind whistled past until . . .

. . . a signal ahead shone RED!

Duffy heaved on the brake and the wheels locked and the
Little Red Train slid along in a shower of sparks and stopped
just an inch away from the end of the line.

Duffy was so tired that he didn't realize he was on a ferry. He knew he had done his best and obeyed signals when they were green and stopped when they were red – so he settled down in his cab for a well-earned snooze.

Duffy woke with a jolt when the ferry docked. He
was told by a rather cross man to get going.

The Little Red Train sped through the night and
the signals shone green all the way.

"Where have you been?" asked Jack the guard when they arrived back at the station.

Duffy shrugged his shoulders. "Your guess is as good as mine," he said, "but it's really good to be home."

The Little Red Train let out a great sigh of steam.

Whoo . . . eee . . . whoo . . . eee . . . eee . . .